dick bruna

miffy
at
school

World International

It's early in the morning, but

Miffy's already gone

walking to school with all her friends

and with her red dress on.

The school was not too far away

they got there very soon

the school looked very cosy and

they had a pretty room.

The teacher got up early too

she stood there at the door

and Miffy was so pleased to see

the pendant that she wore.

The bell was rung to start the day

and school could then begin

when they sat down the teacher saw

that everyone was in.

First we will make a row of curls

said teacher, do your best,

these curls will help you start to write

before you learn the rest.

Then it was time for adding up

and so the teacher drew

two toadstools and another three

Miff did the sum, can you?

They sang a very lovely song

that was their favourite thing

and teacher showed them with her hand

how fast they had to sing.

Then teacher let them build a town

with all the building blocks

with houses, churches and an arch –

there, see how grand it looks.

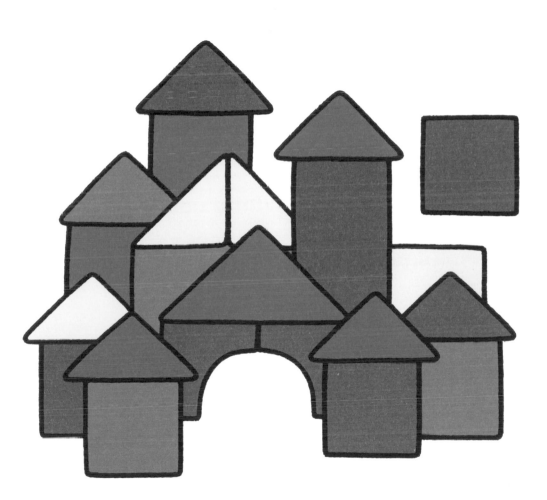

And after that they all ran out

the time for playtime came

and then they danced a little dance

and played a jolly game.

Let's do some drawing, teacher said

and Miff thought that was fine

so first she drew a bright blue sun

a tree, and then a line.

The teacher put the drawings up

they were a splendid sight

a castle, sailing boats, a house

three trees, a plane in flight …

Now everyone sit on the ground

and I will read to you,

said teacher, and they cried, hurrah!

that was exciting, too.

Just as she finished came the bell

they all went home again

the teacher waved to them and called,

see you tomorrow, then!

miffy's library

miffy
miffy goes to stay
miffy is crying
miffy's birthday
miffy at school
miffy's bicycle

miffy's dream
miffy at the zoo
miffy in hospital
miffy in the tent
miffy at the seaside
miffy in the snow

miffy goes flying
miffy at the playground
poppy pig
poppy pig is sick
boris on the mountain
boris in the snow

"nijntje op school"
Original text Dick Bruna 1988 © copyright Mercis Publishing BV.
Illustrations Dick Bruna © copyright Mercis BV 1988.
Published in Great Britain in 1997 by World International Ltd.,
Deanway Technology Centre, Wilmslow Road, Handforth, Cheshire SK9 3FB.
Original English translation © copyright Patricia Crampton 1996.
Publication licensed by Mercis Publishing BV, Amsterdam.
Printed by Sebald Sachsendruck Plauen, Germany. All rights reserved.
ISBN 0-7498-2983-4